Benji goes to the Seaside

Dennis Richards

Illustrated By Jan Gleaves

For Charlie who loved the story of Benji the bus!
Dennis Richards.
Grove Rd School!

Sally the seagull is one of Benji's friends.
You will see her on every page wearing a green scarf.
She is very shy and often hides.
Can you find her?

Published by Grey Street Publishing 2015

ISBN: 978-0-9929764-1-5

Typeset by Skinny Design Ltd.
Printed by Harrogate Printing Ltd.

To order this book please contact: jangleaves1@gmail.com

Benji is a brand new bus,
His paintwork, gleaming and blue.
Big and bold - a double-decker,
He wonders, **“What job will I do?”**

Benji will be the “Coastrider”,
And will have this name for some years.
He has pride of place in the station,
And purrs as he goes through his gears.

Benji goes to the seaside,
Taking families out for the day.

The children excited and happy,
Can't wait to get on their way.

There's Timmy and Tilly and Tessa,
And Jonny and Josie and James.
Danny is sitting with Grandad,
Today there'll be fun and games!

“Upstairs! Upstairs!”

shout the children,
“We want to get the best view.”
Carrying buckets and spades
and their swimsuits,
Delighted to go somewhere new.

“Are we nearly there yet?”

says Tessa,
Before Benji has even left town.
Dad wants to read his paper in peace,
“It’s ages yet… so just settle down!”

Then comes the biggest excitement, as someone has spotted the sea.

"Nearly there!"

yell a number of children, asking Benji "How long will it be?"

The sea sparkles blue in the sunshine,
As Benji prepares for a rest.
Children race to the beach together,
For them this is simply 'The Best'.

Quickly they're in the sea paddling,
They feel they have no time to lose.

Parents are queuing for deckchairs,
For them it's time for a snooze.

Danny makes sure that his Grandad, is safely installed in a chair.

"Go on Danny son, have a paddle, chances like this are so rare."

Benji goes down to the garage,
To get a good wash and a drink.

He must get the children back home now,
This job gives him no time to think.

All too soon the summer is over, and Benji goes back to his base.
It's winter and he stays in the city, the wind and the rain in his face.

He gives of his best through the dark times, looking forward to days in the sun.

Sometimes it snows and he struggles,
But he knows there's a job to be done.

When Easter comes round he is ready, to become a “Coastrider” again.

He sets off as cheerful as ever, but suddenly feels a bad pain.

His engine stutters and splutters as smoke billows up from the floor.
Benji is upset and frightened, as people rush for the door.

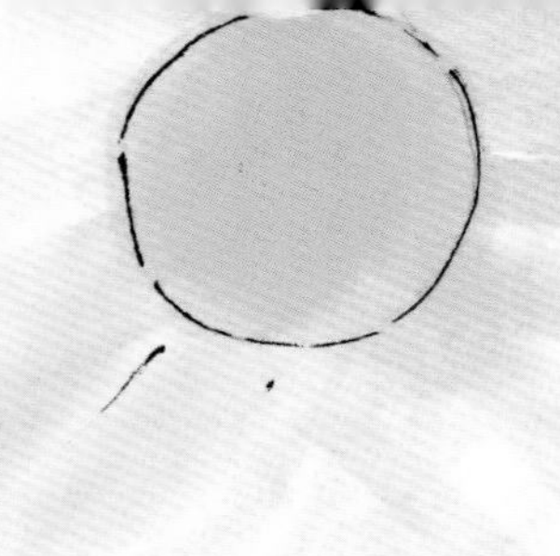

Happily no one is injured, but people are badly delayed.
They're annoyed and cross with poor Benji,
"Just think of the money we've paid!"

All too soon, a brand new "Coastrider",
Resplendent, appears in the yard.

Benji is parked round the corner,
Life has become very hard.

"What happens now?"

thinks Benji.

"I feel old and a bit of a fool…"

"Got just the job!" says his owner,

"You're going to work at a school!"

So Benji now does the school run,
Taking children to learn every day,

To read and do their times tables
And listen to what teachers say.

The children laugh at their school bus,

"Our bus is a tatty old crate!"

No one knows he was once a 'Coastrider'.
Poor Benji is in a bad state.

The Head teacher does
one last duty,
With children at the end
of each day.

Megaphone in hand, he is ready
To see them all safely away.

Danny's Grandad has retired to Seaport, he watches the ships sailing by,
No one bothers to ask him the question,
What he is thinking, and why?

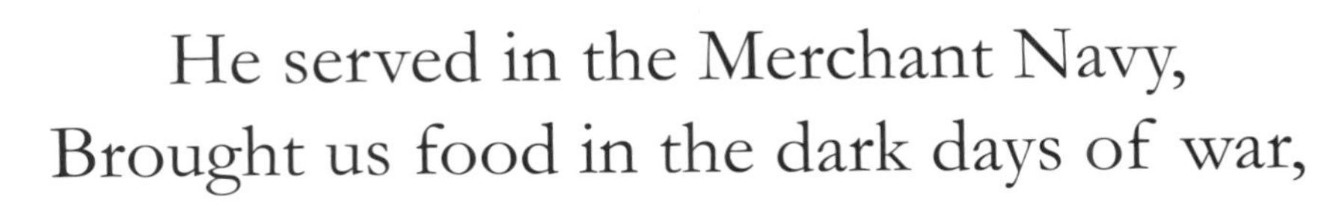

He served in the Merchant Navy,
Brought us food in the dark days of war,

Crossing seas that were fraught with high danger,
Now alone with his thoughts by the shore.

Danny goes over to see him,
Together they look at the views.

"Bus needed for
open-top travel",

Is a headline they read in the news.

Saturday 18th May

The Seaport Gazette

BUS NEEDED FOR OPEN-TOP TRAVEL

Seaport Council met yesterday at the town hall to discuss the need for an open top bus. "The search is now on to find the right bus to do the job" said Councillor Bailey.

"That's just the job for Benji!

He'd love to work here again,
I'll go to the city and find him,
Let's hope I don't search in vain."

Danny finds Benji abandoned,
His schooldays now at an end.

But his engine remains in fine fettle,
There are only a few things to mend.

But Benji must first have a haircut, so passengers can enjoy the sea air.
At first he looks cold and uneasy, but feels better when the
weather is fair.

Next time you see an old bus like Benji, imagine the places he's been!
And think of all the adventures, the towns and the cities he's seen!

Sally the seagull joins Benji, she's not even trying to hide!

Happy to be at the seaside,
Hitching a ride by his side.

The friends are now all together, Danny joins them there too,

They share good times and bad times together,
Exactly what good friends should do!

The End

Dennis Richards is a classroom teacher and Headteacher of many years' experience. He was awarded the OBE for services to education in 2007. He is a prolific writer on education and together with illustrator, Jan Gleaves, published the best-selling "Sylvie on Tour" in 2014.

Dennis Richards and Jan Gleaves also published Sylvie on Tour, a highly acclaimed celebration of the 2014 Grand Depart of the Tour de France.